On Call for You

You

A Sizzling Small-Town Forbidden Romance Between a Protective EMT and His Best Friend's Little Sister

Hana York

Pink Pop Publishing

On Call for You

(Hearts on Duty Book 3)

Copyright © 2025 by Hana York

www.HanaYork.com

Contents

Chapter One

♥

LUCAS

The emergency room pulsed with my favorite kind of mayhem. My heart raced as I maneuvered the stretcher through the sliding doors while my partner's voice cut through the din.

"Male, mid-fifties, went down at the marina!"

Sharp hospital disinfectant stung my nostrils, mixing with the controlled chaos of voices as staff parted the way ahead. I kept one hand steady on the stretcher, the other on the patient's arm—a silent reassurance, even as my mind raced through the vitals, we'd barely managed to stabilize en route.

"BP was 68 over 40," I called out, my voice cutting through the noise. "Pulse is weak but steady now. Couldn't get a clear history before he went out."

"Room three is open," a nurse directed, motioning toward the far end of the ER.

I nodded and moved quickly, my boots squeaking against the linoleum. Just as I reached the exam bay, a petite redhead in scrubs stepped into my path, clipboard in hand and copper curls pinned back beneath a surgical cap.

"Vitals?" she asked, her tone crisp, her gaze flicking from me to the patient.

I blinked. I'd worked with nearly every doctor at Anchor Bay General but didn't recognize her. New. That much was obvious. But the way she took control—calm, efficient like she'd been running this ER for years—caught me off guard.

"BP's holding steady at 92 over 62 now," I said, watching as she leaned over the stretcher, her hands methodical as she assessed the patient. "Pulse is regular but weak. Possible cardiac history, but no confirmation yet."

"Good work stabilizing him." She flashed me a quick, professional smile—businesslike but oddly disarming.

Before I could process why she seemed vaguely familiar, she was already issuing orders. "Push fluids and start a second line," she said to a nurse before turning back to me. "Did he mention any meds or allergies before he lost consciousness?"

"No," I said, shaking my head. "We didn't get that far before he crashed."

Her lips pressed into a thin line as she focused on the patient, her movements efficient as she checked his airway. "Thanks for getting him here in one piece, Carter," she said absently, like she'd memorized my name from my badge.

"Anytime, Doc," I replied, though something about her gave me pause.

She hesitated for a fraction of a second, her emerald eyes flicking up to meet mine. "Sophie," she corrected, her voice professional but not unfriendly. "Just started here last week."

A flicker of something I couldn't quite name settled in my chest.

Sophie.

Recognition tugged at me, but I couldn't place it.

"Lucas," I offered, my gaze lingering on her longer than it should have.

"Nice to meet you, Lucas," she said, turning back to the patient.

I stepped aside, my job done, but my mind wasn't ready to let it go. She was more than competent, but there was something else. A quiet intensity. And just the faintest hint of a chip on her shoulder, like she was ready to prove something.

It shouldn't have mattered. I worked with new doctors all the time.

So why the hell couldn't I shake the feeling that I'd seen her somewhere before?

***

I wound up at The Rusty Anchor that evening, hunched over a drink I'd definitely earned after the day I'd had. The usual bar noise swirled around me—people talking, some twangy country song playing somewhere—but it was all just white noise at that point. My mind was somewhere else.

Or rather, on someone else.

Sophie.

The sharp-eyed redhead from the ER had been stuck in my head all day, and I couldn't decide if it was her confidence, quick hands, or how she'd looked at me like she was trying to figure out a puzzle and I was the missing piece.

I took another sip of my drink, willing the thought away when a familiar voice cut through the noise.

"Lucas!"

I turned just as Nate Whitaker—Detective, best friend, and all-around pain in my ass—grinned his way through the crowded bar and clapped a hand on my shoulder.

"Damn, man, you look like you've been through it today," he said, nodding toward my drink.

"Long shift." I took another sip, not about to mention the part where I couldn't stop thinking about a certain ER doc.

"Well, I got someone you gotta meet," Nate continued, motioning behind him. "My little sister, Sophie. She finally moved back after being away forever."

The glass froze halfway to my lips.

No. Freaking. Way.

I set my drink down very carefully because otherwise, I might drop it.

Sophie.

The redhead from the ER. The woman I'd spent all day trying to forget.

I knew Nate had a sister, but I'd never met her. He'd mentioned her over the years—how she was off at some fancy medical school, how she worked in a big-city hospital, how she was too damn stubborn for her own good. But none of that had prepared me for the woman standing in front of me now.

Sophie's green eyes widened slightly in recognition, but instead of looking shocked, she looked amused. Like she'd already put this together and was just waiting to see how long it would take me to catch up.

"You've got to be kidding me," I muttered, raking a hand through my hair as the pieces clicked into place.

Her lips twitched in that same confident, teasing way I'd seen earlier. "Small world," she said lightly.

"Too small," I muttered.

Nate's brow furrowed as he glanced between us. "Wait a minute. You two know each other?"

Sophie cocked her head nonchalantly. "Oh, we've met. Lucas was the EMT on my first trauma case at Anchor Bay General."

I shifted my weight, keeping my voice steady despite the sudden heat crawling up my neck. "All part of the job."

Nate laughed, completely missing how Sophie and I were still staring at each other. "Look at that—saving me the trouble of introductions."

Yeah. Saving. That was one way to put it.

I flicked my gaze back to Sophie, who looked entirely too pleased with this little twist of fate.

Gorgeous, sharp-witted, and completely off-limits.

Fantastic.

She leaned in slightly, her voice just low enough for only me to hear. "Looks like we'll be seeing a lot more of each other, Lucas."

Her perfume—something light and floral, something that shouldn't make my brain short-circuit but absolutely did—wrapped around me. I swallowed hard, acutely aware of how close she was, how easy it would be to turn my head and...

Nope. Bad idea.

"I guess so," I managed, my voice rougher than I meant for it to be.

Before I could get my bearings, Nate clapped a hand on my back, utterly oblivious to the fact that I was currently having a mild crisis over his sister.

"Hey, I have an idea. Why don't you go with Sophie to her presentation tomorrow?" he suggested. "I've got a case to work, but I don't want her going alone and getting lost."

I opened my mouth to shut that down—because spending more time with Sophie was very clearly a dangerous idea—but she beat me to it.

"That's not necessary," she said quickly. "I'm sure Lucas has better things to do with his time."

Probably. Definitely. I thought to myself.

And yet, I heard myself say, "No, it's fine. I'd be happy to go with you."

Sophie's eyebrows lifted slightly as if she hadn't expected that answer. Hell, neither did I.

Her expression smoothed just as quickly, her voice carefully neutral. "Well, if you're sure. It's at one of the elementary schools on the outskirts of town."

I shifted my weight, fighting the ridiculous mix of nerves and anticipation curling in my gut. "I know exactly where that is. How's 8:30 tomorrow morning sound?"

Then she smiled. Not just any smile—one that hit me like a gut punch, slow and knowing like she already had me figured out.

"Perfect," she said, reaching for her phone. "I'll text you my address."

Great. Just great.

Tomorrow, I'd be spending the day alone with Sophie Whitaker.

I'd faced down my share of life-threatening moments, but hanging out with Nate's sister alone? Now that was the kind of trouble I wasn't trained for.

Chapter Two

♥

SOPHIE

A light drizzle tapped against the windshield as Lucas guided the ambulance down the winding country road. I flipped through the laminated first-aid charts we planned to use for the elementary school presentation, but my attention kept drifting to the man behind the wheel.

Lucas Carter.

My brother's best friend.

Someone I'd heard about for years but had only just met.

And now we were stuck in an ambulance together, just the two of us, with nothing but an hour's drive and a thunderstorm rolling in to keep us company.

"You're awfully quiet for someone about to inspire a room full of future medics," I teased, tilting my head to watch him.

Lucas glanced at me, one brow lifting. "Inspire, huh? I thought we were just trying to keep them from swallowing marbles or sticking forks in outlets."

I laughed, shutting the charts. "You're selling yourself short, Carter. Who knows? You might convince a kid to join EMS."

"Right." His voice was dry, but I caught the subtle twitch at the corner of his mouth like he was trying not to smile. "And you'll be dazzling them with your medical brilliance."

I grinned. "Or terrifying them with anatomy charts. Either way, they'll remember us."

He shook his head, but I swore I saw the ghost of a smirk. Interesting.

Before I could push my luck, thunder rumbled in the distance, and the drizzle turned into a sudden downpour.

Lucas cranked the wipers to full speed, but the rain was relentless, a heavy sheet blurring the road ahead. His fingers tightened on the wheel, his usual calm turning laser-focused.

"Mother Nature's really outdoing herself," he muttered.

"No kidding." I peered through the storm, barely making out the winding road. "Maybe we should head back?"

"Past that point now." His voice was steady, but I could feel the shift in the air—the sharpness of his attention, the way he braced himself like he was preparing for the worst. "We'll just take it slow."

Lightning split the sky, a jagged streak of white-hot electricity, followed by a thunderclap that rattled through my chest. Lucas didn't even flinch.

Then, as we rounded a bend, the headlights illuminated a massive tree sprawled across the road, its roots ripped clean from the earth.

Lucas slammed on the brakes.

The ambulance skidded slightly, tires splashing against the slick pavement before stopping just feet from the obstruction.

I let out a slow breath, staring at the fallen tree through the rain-streaked windshield.

"Well," I said, trying to sound unbothered, "that's inconvenient."

Static crackled through the radio as Lucas called in our location and the roadblock.

The dispatcher's weary voice listed off similar reports coming in—downed trees, flooded streets, emergency crews stretched thin. It didn't take a genius to figure out we weren't getting out of here anytime soon.

"Any idea when we can get this cleared?" Lucas asked, though I could already tell he wouldn't like the answer.

"Looking at a few hours minimum," came the reply, heavy with exhaustion.

Lucas exhaled sharply, gripping the wheel. He glanced at me, his expression unreadable. "There's a ranger station about half a mile back. We can wait it out there."

I shut the supply box, shifting in my seat. "Better than sitting here."

Lucas didn't respond, just threw the ambulance into reverse, maneuvering carefully before turning us around. The windshield wipers fought against the downpour, but the road ahead was barely visible through the sheets of rain.

Lucas kept both hands firm on the wheel, his jaw tight as he navigated the slick road. Water pooled along the edges, the tires splashing through deep puddles, making every turn feel unsteady. The trees lining the road swayed violently, their branches bending under the force of the wind.

The headlights finally caught on a break in the tree line—the ranger station.

Lucas eased the ambulance into the small gravel lot, the engine rumbling as he threw it into park. The building stood just ahead, small but sturdy, a single-room cabin built to withstand the elements.

He turned to me, rain hammering the roof above us. "Ready to make a run for it?"

I exhaled, tugging my jacket tighter. "Not really, but I don't think we have much of a choice."

Lucas smirked. "Then let's go."

I nodded, pulling my jacket tighter as we stepped into the storm. The wind howled around us, rain soaking through my clothes in seconds. By the time we reached the small wooden cabin, I was drenched, my curls plastered to my face.

Lucas pushed open the door and held it for me, his broad frame blocking most of the rain. I stepped inside, instantly shivering at the contrast between the warmth of the space and the icy chill still clinging to my skin.

"Not bad," I said, wringing out my rain-soaked jacket and glancing around. "Rustic, but it'll do."

Lucas grabbed a lantern from the shelf, turning it on. A soft glow spread through the cabin, bouncing off the wooden walls.

"It's not the Ritz, but at least it's dry."

I huffed out a small laugh, shaking out my damp curls. "I'll take it."

Outside, the storm raged on, wind shrieking against the windows, rain hammering the glass. I dug through a supply box, emerging with a flashlight, a pack of crackers, and a couple of mylar emergency blankets which we gratefully wrapped around ourselves.

"Five-star dining right here," I said dryly, tearing open the wrapper and holding it out to Lucas.

He took a few with a slight smile, watching me a little too closely like he was trying to figure something out. It made my stomach dip in a way I wasn't ready to analyze.

"You always this resourceful?" he asked, popping a cracker into his mouth.

"Part of the job." I leaned against the table, stretching out my damp limbs. "Doctors learn to improvise."

Lucas nodded, but his gaze lingered, a little too perceptive.

"You've got good instincts," he said after a pause.

The unexpected compliment caught me off guard. My fingers stilled against the supply box. "Thanks."

I kept my tone light, but something in his voice made my chest tighten.

"I wish everyone at the hospital thought so," I admitted, glancing away. "It's hard enough proving myself without being underestimated on sight."

Lucas frowned. "You mean because you're—"

"Because I'm small," I cut in, unable to mask my irritation. "And because some people expect me to be selling cookies rather than running a trauma bay."

Lucas's expression darkened.

"I had one attending who called me 'Little Red' for a month," I said, rolling my eyes. "It took shutting him down in front of the entire team to stop it."

Lucas's brow creased. "Hold up—you're telling me people seriously underestimate you that often?"

I let out a short laugh. "Like clockwork." I shrugged, trying to shake it off. "Same old story. At least my work holds up."

Lucas's jaw tightened. "That's complete bullshit."

His voice was sharp, edged with something that made my breath hitch.

"If they can't see how good you are, they're not worth losing sleep over."

Something about how he said it—firm, matter-of-fact like there was no doubt in his mind—made warmth spread through my chest.

I'd spent years fighting for respect. Proving my place.

I wasn't used to someone just... believing in me.

Especially not someone like him.

Chapter Three

♥

LUCAS

The storm raged on outside, rain hammering against the cabin roof, but inside, it was quiet. Too quiet.

I should have been thinking about the road conditions. About how long we'd be stuck here. About anything but Sophie Whitaker.

But that was the problem.

With nowhere else to focus, my attention kept drifting—to the way she moved around the space so effortlessly, the damp curls framing her face, and the way the lantern's glow softened the sharp edges of her features.

I told myself I wasn't looking.

That I was just keeping an eye on her, the way I would with anyone riding out a storm in a cabin with me.

But that was a lie.

The lantern's glow flickered across her face, casting soft shadows over her features, tracing the curves I had no business noticing. She's taken off the emergency blanket and her wet clothes clung to her in ways that made it impossible not to notice. Made it impossible not to wonder what it would feel like to trace those curves with my hands. To pull her close, feel the heat of her body against mine, kiss her just once—just to see if it was as good as my brain was already trying to convince me it would be.

I clenched my jaw and shook the thought loose before it could take root. Jesus, Carter. Get a grip.

She was Nate's little sister.

And that made her off-limits.

Why did *that* feel like the biggest lie I'd ever told myself?

Sophie cleared her throat, dragging me out of my own head. "So," she said, tilting her head slightly, "how long have you been an EMT?"

Grateful for the distraction, I leaned back against the cabin wall, forcing myself to focus on the conversation instead of how damn good she looked standing in front of me.

"Going on eight years now," I replied, my voice lower than I intended. "Can't imagine doing anything else."

"What made you want to be an EMT?" Her voice softened like she actually cared about the answer.

I exhaled slowly, running a hand through my damp hair. "My mom," I said after a moment. "She was a nurse. She used to come home after long shifts and tell me stories—about the people she helped, the lives she saved. I guess it just stuck."

Sophie's expression shifted, something warm and understanding flashing in her emerald eyes. "She must be proud."

I swallowed, my chest tightening. "She was." I paused, forcing the words out. "She passed a few years ago, but... yeah, I think was happy with where I ended up."

"I'm sure she was more than happy," Sophie murmured, her voice full of conviction. "I have no doubt she was proud, Lucas."

Her sincerity made something in my chest twist. Our eyes met, and for the first time since stepping into this cabin, I forgot about the storm outside.

I forgot about Nate.

I forgot about every reason I shouldn't be standing this close to her, wanting her the way I did.

Sophie stepped forward, closing the space between us before I could think to move away. She reached out, her fingers brushing my arm—light, warm, grounding.

"I'm sorry about your mom," she said softly. "She sounds like an amazing woman."

I barely felt the words because all I could feel was her touch.

It was barely there, but my body reacted like she'd set me on fire.

I forced a rough breath, my voice not nearly as steady as I wanted. "She was."

And then Sophie looked at me.

Really looked at me.

Like she saw past the careful walls I kept up. Like she saw how my pulse hammered and how my restraint was fraying right in front of her.

Thunder rolled in the distance, but all I could hear was my heart pounding.

"Lucas," she whispered.

I should have stepped back.

Should have ended this before it even started.

But I didn't.

Because in this moment, Sophie wasn't just Nate's little sister. She was the woman I couldn't get out of my head—even though I'd only known her for a handful of days. The woman standing in front of me, looking at me like she wanted this just as much as I did.

I swallowed hard, barely recognizing my own voice when I finally spoke. "Sophie... we shouldn't."

She tilted her head slightly, her lips curving into something shy of a smile. "We probably shouldn't," she murmured, her voice teasing, daring me to deny her. "But god, I want to."

And just like that, my restraint snapped.

A rough sound left my throat as I closed the space between us, pulling her flush against me.

My hands found her instantly—one threading into her damp copper hair, the other gripping her waist, anchoring her to me.

Sophie melted into me like we'd done this a hundred times before.

Like she belonged there.

And for the first time in years, I didn't care if I was making a mistake.

Because this?

This felt inevitable.

Sophie's lips met mine with a hunger that matched my own. Her fingers tangled in my hair, pulling me closer as she arched against me. I groaned, deepening the kiss, tasting rain and desire on her tongue.

My fingers traced down her back, following her spine's gentle curve. A shiver ran through Sophie as I guided her against the cabin wall. The lantern light played across her face, her flushed skin glowing, those emerald eyes dark with desire.

"Lucas," she whispered, the word catching in her throat.

I rested my forehead against hers, my breath coming fast. "We should stop," I said softly, even while every part of me ached to continue.

Sophie's fingers traced along my jaw, her touch feather-light but searing. "Do you want to stop?"

I swallowed hard, knowing I should say yes. That we should end this before it went any further. But the words caught in my throat as I gazed into her eyes, dark with desire.

"No," I admitted roughly. "God help me, I don't want to stop."

Sophie's lips curved into a slow, sensual smile. "Then don't," she whispered, her breath warm against my skin.

That was all it took for my remaining self-control to crumble.

I captured her mouth in a searing kiss, pouring all my pent-up longing into it. Sophie moaned softly, her body melting against mine as her fingers raked through my hair.

I growled low in my throat, pressing her more firmly against the wall. Sophie's legs wrapped around my waist as I lifted her, her damp clothes clinging to her curves.

My hands slid under Sophie's rain-soaked shirt, tracing the soft skin of her waist. She shivered at my touch, arching into me with a breathy moan that sent heat coursing through my veins. I kissed a trail down her neck, tasting rainwater and desire on her flushed skin.

I pulled back just enough to meet her gaze, searching her eyes for any sign of hesitation. But all I saw was raw need reflecting back at me, matching the ache in my chest.

Sophie's hands found the hem of my shirt, tugging insistently. "Off," she commanded, her voice husky.

I obliged, quickly stripping off the damp fabric. Sophie's eyes roamed hungrily over my bare chest, her fingers tracing the lines of muscle.

"God, you're gorgeous," she breathed, leaning in to press hot, open-mouthed kisses along my chest.

I groaned, my hands sliding under Sophie's shirt and up her sides. "Look who's talking," I murmured, my voice husky with desire. With one smooth motion, I pulled her shirt up and off, revealing a lace bra that made my mind go blank.

I stared at Sophie, transfixed by the delicate fabric against her fair skin and the rapid rise and fall of her chest. My hands slid up to cup her breasts through the delicate material. Sophie leaned into me with a quiet moan.

Slowly, reverently, I lowered my head to press a kiss to the swell of her breast just above the lace. My lips were warm and soft against her skin, sending shivers down her spine. I trailed kisses along the edge of her bra, my stubble lightly scraping her sensitive flesh.

Sophie's fingers tangled in my hair, holding me close as I lavished attention on her breasts. I nuzzled the valley between them, inhaling her intoxicating scent - a mix of rain and something uniquely Sophie. My hands slid around to her back, fingers deftly unhooking her bra.

As the lace fell away, I paused to drink in the sight of her. Sophie's breasts were perfect - soft and full, with rosy peaks already tightened with arousal. I cupped them gently, thumbs brushing over her sensitive nipples.

Sophie gasped at my touch, her back arching to press herself more firmly into my hands. The rough calluses on my palms skimmed over her soft skin, and for a fleeting second, I worried—worried that my hands, hardened from years in the field, might be too rough for her.

But then she shivered and pulled me closer, like she craved the friction, like she wanted more.

I lowered my head, capturing one peaked nipple between my lips. My tongue swirled around the sensitive bud as Sophie moaned softly, and I moved to the other breast sucking her nipple into my mouth until she was squirming.

"Lucas," she breathed, her voice husky with need. "Please..."

I trailed my hands down Sophie's sides, my fingertips following the curve of her waist until they found the edge of her pants. Our eyes locked, my gaze asking what my voice didn't. Sophie nodded and I eased her pants down. The lace panties she wore underneath matched her bra, the delicate fabric a stark contrast against her pale skin. My eyes locked onto her, utterly captivated. I brushed my lips against her hip in a gentle kiss before easing her panties down. Sophie's gaze traveled over me with unmistakable want.

"Your turn," she murmured, a wicked glint in her eye.

Her hands found my belt, deftly unbuckling it. The soft clink of metal sent a jolt of anticipation through me. Sophie's fingers brushed against my stomach as she undid the button of my jeans, then slowly lowered the zipper.

I sucked in a sharp breath as her hand ghosted over the bulge straining against my boxers. Sophie's lips curved into a knowing smile as she pushed my jeans down my hips. I kicked them off, leaving me in just my underwear.

Sophie's fingers traced the waistband of my boxers, her touch feather-light and teasing. She looked up at me through her lashes, her green eyes dark with desire. Slowly, torturously, she hooked her thumbs under the elastic and began to slide the fabric down.

I held my breath as Sophie revealed me inch by agonizing inch. The cool air of the cabin kissed my heated skin, making me shiver. Sophie's gaze was fixed downward, watching intently as she eased my boxers over my hips and thighs.

When I finally sprang free, Sophie's eyes widened slightly. She licked her lips, a small gesture that sent fire racing through my veins. Her fingers ghosted along my length, exploring with gossamer-soft touches that made my muscles clench.

"God, Lucas," she breathed, wrapping her hand around me.

Sophie's fingers wrapped around me, her touch electric. She looked up, her emerald eyes dark with desire as she slowly sank to her knees. My breath caught in my throat at the sight of her, naked and beautiful, gazing up at me with raw hunger.

Sophie leaned in, her breath warm against my sensitive skin. She pressed a soft kiss to my hip, then trailed her lips lower. I shuddered as she nuzzled the base of my shaft, inhaling deeply.

"You smell so good," she murmured, her voice husky. "I want to taste you."

Before I could respond, Sophie leaned forward and ran her tongue along my length in one long, torturous stroke. A groan tore from my throat, my hands instinctively threading into her copper curls.

Sophie's lips curved into a wicked smile as she swirled her tongue around the tip of my cock, teasing and exploring. Her hand stroked me slowly as she lavished attention on the sensitive head, alternating between feather-light licks and firm swirls of her tongue.

When she finally took me into her mouth, the wet heat nearly undid me. I groaned, my fingers tightening in her hair as she took me deeper. Sophie hollowed her cheeks, sucking firmly as she bobbed her head.

The sight of her lips wrapped around me, combined with the exquisite sensation of her mouth, was almost too much. I fought to keep my hips still, to let her set the pace. But when Sophie looked up at me through her lashes, her emerald eyes dark with desire, my control slipped.

My hips jerked forward, pushing deeper into her mouth.

"Sophie," I growled, my voice rough with desire. "God, that feels incredible."

She hummed in response, the vibrations sending shock-waves of pleasure through me.

Sophie's lips and tongue worked me with exquisite skill, bringing me closer and closer to the edge. The wet heat of her mouth combined with the suction and the sight of her on her knees before me was almost too much to bear. I could feel the pressure building, my muscles tensing as I neared release.

My fingers tightened in her copper curls, guiding her movements as the pressure built. Her tongue swirled around the sensitive head before she took me deep again, her throat relaxing to accommodate my full length.

"Sophie," I gasped, my voice ragged. "I'm close..."

Her hand wrapped around the base of my shaft, stroking in time with the bobbing of her head. The dual sensation was overwhelming.

My hips jerked involuntarily as she cupped and gently squeezed my balls, adding another layer of sensation that had me seeing stars. I couldn't tear my eyes away from the sight of her lips stretched around me, her cheeks hollowed as she sucked.

Sophie's movements became more insistent, her tongue swirling and stroking as she took me deeper, pushing me over the edge. With a guttural groan, I came hard, my hips jerking as waves of pleasure crashed over me.

Sophie moaned softly, swallowing every drop as she continued to suck and lick, drawing out my orgasm until I was trembling. When she finally pulled away, she looked up at me with hooded eyes, her lips swollen and glistening. The sight of her like that, flushed and disheveled because of me, sent another jolt of arousal through my body.

I reached down, gently cupping her face in my hands as I pulled her to her feet. My lips found hers in a searing kiss, tasting myself on her lips.

I broke the kiss, my breath ragged as I gazed into her eyes. "My turn," I murmured, my voice husky with desire.

Sophie's lips curved into a sultry smile. "Oh?" she breathed, her tone teasing. "And what exactly did you have in mind?"

Instead of answering, I moved her back against the table and slowly sank to my knees before her, my hands trailing down her sides. Sophie's breath hitched as I pressed a reverent kiss to her hip bone, then trailed my lips across her lower abdomen. Her skin was impossibly soft under my touch, flushed with arousal.

I looked up at her, drinking in the sight of her naked form bathed in the lantern's warm glow. Her copper curls fell in damp waves around her face, her eyes dark with need. She was breathtaking.

"I want to taste every inch of you," I murmured.

Chapter Four

❤

Sophie

A sharp burst of static cut through the air as Lucas' emergency radio blared to life, the dispatcher's voice cutting through the heated atmosphere.

"All available units, we have a multi-vehicle pileup on Highway 9. Multiple injuries reported. Anchor Bay General is calling in all staff."

Simultaneously, my pager began beeping insistently from my discarded pants. I pulled away from Lucas, my eyes wide as I scrambled to retrieve it.

"Shit," I muttered, scanning the message that had just come through. Mass event. They need all hands on deck.

Lucas ran a hand through his hair, his frustration sharp, but it lasted only a second before duty took over. "Damn it. We have to go."

The heat from moments ago evaporated, replaced by the familiar snap of adrenaline. No time to think about anything except the job. I fumbled with the buttons of my shirt, my fingers shaking slightly, but not from the storm raging outside.

Lucas grabbed the radio, already shifting into EMT mode. "This is Carter. I'm with Dr. Whitaker, about two miles out from the accident site. Tree blocking the road, but we can get around on foot. ETA twenty minutes."

"Copy that, Carter," came the dispatcher's reply. "Be careful out there."

Lucas and I exchanged a look—no hesitation, no doubt. We knew what had to be done.

We moved fast, grabbing our clothes in the dim lantern light, the air between us still thick with everything that had happened—and everything that now had to be pushed aside.

I yanked my damp shirt over my shoulders, fingers fumbling with it even as my brain snapped into work mode. Focus. Dress. Move.

Lucas was doing the same, shrugging into his uniform with the kind of practiced efficiency that came from years on the job.

"Boots," he muttered, shoving his feet into his and grabbing his jacket in one motion.

I nodded, already lacing mine up with quick, precise movements. Seconds mattered.

Lucas slung his gear over his shoulder and reached for the door. "Let's move."

I exhaled, shoving aside every stray thought that had nothing to do with the mass casualty waiting for us down the road.

Back to work. Back to reality.

I nodded once. "Let's move."

We pushed out into the storm. The rain had faded to a drizzle, but the wind still cut through my damp clothes as we sprinted for the ambulance.

"Grab whatever you can carry!" Lucas called over the gusts. "Could be anything waiting for us out there."

I was already running through the checklist in my head, mentally categorizing supplies. We wouldn't have the luxury of returning for anything we forgot.

When we reached the ambulance, Lucas yanked the back doors open, and the sterile antiseptic scent hit me. The rig's usual orderly calm shattered into electric tension.

"Get the trauma kit," I called out, my hand already on the red duffel. "I'll handle IVs and fluids."

Like a well-oiled machine, we fell into our roles. No hesitation. No missteps. Just pure instinct from countless hours of practice taking command.

Lucas slung the heavy trauma kit over his shoulder, then grabbed a backpack and began stuffing it with additional supplies. I scanned the shelves, moving on instinct.

Portable defibrillator? Check. Cervical collars? Check. Gauze, bandages, antiseptics? More than enough.

We loaded up, knowing each item could mean the difference between life and death.

Lucas adjusted his pack with steady hands, though tension crackled between us. "Ready?"

I caught his gaze. Saw the steel there. The focus.

"Let's go."

We pressed on, maneuvering around the fallen tree onto muddy ground. Wind tore at our clothes, fighting to drag us back. Darkness swallowed the road ahead, but the approaching sirens drove us forward.

Lucas kept pace beside me, his movements efficient and controlled, while I focused on the weight of the medical bags digging into my shoulders. I wasn't as big as him but matched his stride without hesitation. No way was I slowing down.

The ground turned treacherous, mud sucking at my boots as we moved through the thick brush, each step heavier than the last. But then, as we reached the top of the hill, we both froze.

Below us, the highway was barely recognizable—a scene of twisted metal, shattered glass, and flashing red and blue lights cutting through the darkness.

Amid the wreckage, some people staggered through the chaos while others lay still, unmoving. Smoke curled into the sky, the acrid scent of gasoline and burnt rubber sharp enough to sting my nose.

"Jesus," I whispered, the sheer scale of it pressing in on me.

Lucas's jaw tightened. "Come on," he muttered, his voice steady but hard. "We need to find incident command and get to work."

I forced down the lump in my throat. This wasn't the time to freeze. This was what I'd trained for.

Without another word, we broke into a jog, weaving through the wreckage toward the heart of the disaster.

Time blurred as we threw ourselves into the chaos, moving from patient to patient, assessing injuries, stabilizing the critically wounded, and coordinating with other first responders. The scene was raw and overwhelming, but I didn't have the luxury of feeling any of it.

Not yet.

All that mattered was keeping people alive.

I moved on instinct.

IVs inserted. Pressure bandages secured. Orders fired off to the EMTs working beside me. There was no time to hesitate, no time to second-guess. The chaos blurred around me, but my hands were steady, my focus locked onto each patient in front of me.

The rain hadn't let up, soaking through my scrubs, and stray curls clung to my forehead, damp and unruly. I barely noticed. The only thing that mattered was keeping people alive.

Somewhere nearby, Lucas was doing the heavy lifting—literally. I caught glimpses of him through the rain and flashing emergency lights, wrenching doors off crushed cars, hauling victims on backboards through the mud, his uniform darkened with sweat and rain. He never stopped, never slowed, muscles straining as he worked through pure force of will.

I should have been focusing solely on my patients. But every time I looked up, my eyes found him.

And every time, he was already looking back.

By the time the last ambulance pulled away, the sky had started bleeding into dusk, warm hues mixing with the remnants of storm clouds. The chaos of the accident scene was behind us, but it still clung to my skin—the mud, the sweat, the blood that wasn't mine.

Lucas and I hitched a ride back to the ER, too drained for conversation. The automatic doors slid open with a soft hiss, ushering us into the familiar smell of disinfectant and the harsh glare of overhead lights.

The post-shift crash was hitting hard. The kind of exhaustion that didn't just settle in your muscles but burrowed deep into your bones. Adrenaline gone. Limbs heavy.

I caught a glimpse of my reflection in one of the glass panels—a frizzy halo of curls, dark half-moons under my eyes—but my pulse still thrummed with something lighter. We'd done it. We'd kept death at bay, at least for today.

Lucas and I trudged toward the staff lounge, neither willing to face the mountain of paperwork just yet.

Thank God—an empty lounge.

Lucas dropped onto the battered old couch with a dramatic exhale, rubbing a hand down his face. I grabbed two mugs from the shelf and headed straight toward the coffee pot. My hands shook slightly as I poured, the come-down from the high of the last few hours catching up to me.

"Here," I said softly, passing one to Lucas before sinking onto the couch beside him. "You look like you need this as much as I do."

He took the mug, our fingers brushing. Even through the exhaustion, the contact sent a slight jolt through me—a spark I hadn't thought I'd have the energy to feel.

Lucas took a long sip, letting the bitter liquid pull him back to life. "You were amazing out there," he murmured, turning to look at me.

Our eyes met, and I felt something lift despite the weight pressing down on my body.

"*You* were incredible back there," I countered, shifting slightly to face him. "That one man was panicking, but you talked him through it like you'd known him for years. I've never seen someone handle a scene like that."

Lucas shrugged, but I didn't miss how my words settled into him. "Come on, it's what we're trained for."

"Stop being modest," I said, leaning forward slightly. "It's different with you, Lucas. You've got a way with people. The calm you bring to chaos—that's not something they teach in training."

His lips parted slightly like he wasn't sure how to respond. For a guy who usually had a witty retort for everything, that moment of hesitation said more than words could.

Heat crept up his neck, but when he finally spoke, his voice was quieter. "Thanks." His fingers tapped against his mug before he glanced back at me. "You were pretty incredible yourself, Dr. Whitaker. The way you took charge, coordinating triage... I've worked with attendings who couldn't have handled that scene half as well."

A slow smile tugged at my lips, the day's weight momentarily forgotten. "Well, I did have some pretty decent backup."

Lucas huffed out a soft laugh, shaking his head.

The storm was over. But I wasn't sure how to explain the one still brewing between us.

My hands curled around the empty coffee mug, the warmth long gone, but I barely noticed. My thoughts were too tangled—wrapped around everything that had happened, everything that almost happened.

Beside me, Lucas sat tense and quiet, his broad shoulders rigid, his jaw tight. The space between us felt charged, like something unspoken still hung in the air, waiting to be acknowledged.

I turned to him, forcing myself to break the silence. "Lucas," I said softly, meeting his gaze. "About what happened in the cabin..."

He lifted a hand, cutting me off gently. "Sophie," he murmured, his voice rough, like the words hurt to say.

"What happened in that cabin... it was incredible. You're incredible."

I swallowed hard, my heart hammering against my ribs.

"I've never felt anything like that before," he admitted, dragging a hand through his hair like he was barely holding himself together. His jaw clenched, his next words forced out like they physically pained him. "But Sophie, as much as I want this, I... I can't. You're Nate's little sister."

The air went still. The weight of those words crushed down on me.

I shook my head, my stomach twisting. "What does that have to do with anything?"

Lucas exhaled sharply, rubbing a hand down his face. "Nate's my best friend. He's like a brother to me. And you... you're his little sister."

There it was.

Of all the ways he made me feel seen, wanted, known—this was the one place he refused to see me for who I was. Not as a woman, not as someone who had just given herself to him in the most intimate way possible. Just Nate's sister.

I stiffened, something inside me cracking.

His fingers brushed my cheek, lingering for just a second too long—like he didn't want to let go. But then he did.

He pulled away, retreating like what we'd done, what we *were*, was a mistake.

"I can't get involved with you," he said quietly. "No matter how much I want to. It would complicate everything."

Anger, hurt, and frustration slammed into me all at once, burning hot in my chest.

"Stop acting like this is just about Nate," I snapped, stepping closer, refusing to let him hide behind my brother. "This is about you. You're the one too afraid to see where this could go."

His whole body went rigid, like I'd struck him. But I didn't care. Because maybe I had finally seen him clearly too.

"You felt it too," I pressed, my voice softer now but no less confident. "Whatever this is between us, it's not something you can just brush aside."

Lucas's defenses wavered. I could see how his breathing shifted, and his hand curled into a fist like he was physically trying to hold himself back.

"Sophie, I..."

"No." I cut him off, my hand pressing against his chest, right over his heart. His pulse thundered beneath my palm, hard and fast, just like mine.

"I get that you're worried about Nate's reaction. But this isn't about him. It's about us."

Lucas swallowed hard, torn. I could feel it in every line of his body—the pull toward me, the hesitation, the war raging inside him.

"I felt something in that cabin," I whispered, voice raw. "Something I've never experienced before. Are you really willing to walk away from that because of my brother?"

Lucas let out a sharp breath, closing his eyes for half a second as if trying to steady himself.

"God, Sophie," he muttered. "Being with you was... incredible. But Nate—"

"Nate doesn't get a say in who I date. He doesn't dictate my life," I interrupted firmly. "And he sure as hell doesn't get to dictate yours."

Lucas hesitated. Torn between loyalty and desire.

I leaned closer, tilting my head and holding his gaze. "Tell me you don't feel this," I whispered. "Tell me I'm imagining it, and I'll drop it right now."

His hand covered mine, fingers wrapping over my knuckles. He didn't push me away. Didn't let go. Instead, his thumb brushed softly against my skin, sending heat curling through me.

His voice was hoarse, full of something raw and unsteady. "I can't."

My heart skipped a beat.

"What I feel for you..." He exhaled hard, shaking his head like he couldn't quite believe it. "It's unlike anything I've ever experienced."

Relief and anticipation tangled together, but before I could speak, he added, "But I need to talk to Nate first."

I studied him for a long moment. His stubbornness. His damn loyalty.

Finally, I nodded. "I get it. Nate means the world to both of us." I let my fingers trail lightly over his chest before I pulled away. "Just... don't let that stop you from taking a chance on something special."

Then, before he could overthink it, I leaned in, pressing a soft kiss to his cheek.

Pulling back, I let my lips graze close enough to his ear to murmur, "Though try not to overthink it. I've never been good at waiting. Don't let your doubts stop you from taking a chance on something special."

And with that, I left him there to feel the weight of my words. The weight of what we both knew was inevitable.

Chapter Five

♥

LUCAS

The streets of Anchor Bay were quiet and empty, the kind of stillness that usually settled my mind. Not tonight.

I drove on autopilot, but my thoughts were stuck on everything that had happened today—the morning at the cabin, the chaos of the accident site, the exhaustion that clung to my bones.

And, more than anything, Sophie's words.

"Don't let your doubts stop you from taking a chance on something special."

I let out a heavy breath, knuckles white on the steering wheel as I turned into the driveway. My porch light pierced the night, stretching shadows over the old wooden steps.

Usually, getting home felt like a weight lifting. Tonight just left me hollow. Incomplete.

Stepping out of my truck, the scent of salt air and blooming jasmine wrapped around me, a familiar part of Anchor Bay that I usually found comforting. But tonight, it felt off—bittersweet in a way I couldn't quite name.

I moved on instinct, flicking on the lights as I stepped inside. The living room was just as I left it—warm, lived-in, but empty in a way I never noticed.

The well-worn leather couch sat waiting, the bookshelf overflowing with medical texts and paperbacks I kept meaning to read. A framed photo of my mom rested on the side table, her kind eyes watching me like she could see the thoughts I was trying to shove down.

I ran a hand through my hair, exhaling as I shrugged off my jacket. My muscles ached, stiff from hours of strain from lifting, running, and carrying. I kicked off my mud-caked boots by the door, tossed my keys onto the table, and headed straight for the shower.

Hot water pounded against my shoulders, easing some of the tension but doing nothing to clear my head.

Because I wasn't just thinking about today.

I was thinking about her.

Sophie.

The way her copper curls slipped loose from her pony-tail, framing her face as she worked. The way her voice cut through the chaos at the accident scene—calm, commanding, steady when everyone else was barely holding it together.

The way she made me feel something I thought I had no business feeling.

I let out a rough breath, bracing my hands against the tile. This shouldn't be happening.

She was off-limits.

She was Nate's little sister.

But none of that changed the fact that she was also the one person I couldn't get out of my head.

I groaned, pressing my forehead against the cool tile. As if that would do anything to drown out the memories.

But they came anyway—flooding in, sharp and relentless.

The way Sophie felt beneath my hands, soft and warm, her skin like silk against my fingertips.

The way she looked up at me through her lashes, emerald eyes dark with need, before taking me into her mouth.

Jesus.

A fresh wave of heat rolled through me, warring against the cold tile. Guilt followed close behind.

I wanted Sophie. God, how I wanted her. But right on the heels of that undeniable truth came another—the thought of Nate.

Of what he'd say if he knew.

Of how badly I'd be betraying his trust.

I exhaled hard and shut off the water, stepping out of the shower before I could let my thoughts spiral further.

Grabbing a towel, I dragged it over my face, then across my chest, before securing it around my waist. I swiped my palm over the fogged mirror, my reflection emerging—dark eyes filled with something I didn't want to name.

This push and pull, this war between what I wanted and what was right, had to stop.

With a frustrated sigh, I padded into my bedroom, pulling on a pair of worn sweatpants and an old t-shirt before collapsing onto the bed.

Sleep didn't come easy.

Not when my mind wouldn't shut the hell up.

Not when every moment with Sophie played on a loop behind my eyes.

I groaned, throwing an arm over my face.

I needed to talk to Nate.

To clear the air.

To figure out what the hell I was supposed to do about Sophie Whitaker.

Because pretending she wasn't getting under my skin?

That wasn't an option anymore.

I stared at my phone, thumb hovering over Nate's name. For a long second, I hesitated.

Once I hit call, there was no taking it back.

With a sharp exhale, I pressed the button.

The phone barely rang twice before Nate picked up. "Lucas? Everything okay, man?"

I swallowed, my throat suddenly dry. "Yeah, I'm fine. Listen, Nate... we need to talk. Can you meet me at The Rusty Anchor in an hour?"

A pause. Too long for comfort.

"Sure," Nate finally said, concern creeping into his tone. "Everything good?"

Not even close.

"Yeah," I lied. "See you soon."

I got to The Rusty Anchor early but barely noticed the usual comforts of the place.

Music hummed through the speakers; the scent of grease and stale beer clung to the air, but none of it helped quiet the chaos in my head.

How was this going to go?

Would Nate understand? Could our friendship survive this?

Was Sophie worth the risk?

I tapped my fingers against the worn table, the anxious rhythm mirroring the churn in my gut. I already knew the answer to that last question.

Yes.

The door swung open, and Nate walked in, his sharp gaze scanning the room until he found me. He frowned, heading over, worry lines already etched into his forehead.

"Hey," Nate said, dropping into the booth with a squeak of old vinyl. "That call had me worried. Everything okay?"

I drew in a deep breath to steady my nerves.

"Listen, Nate." The words came out barely above a whisper. "It's about Sophie."

His face went rigid. "Sophie? What happened?"

"She's fine," I said quickly, holding up a hand. "It's not like that."

Nate's jaw ticked as he studied me. "Then what is it?"

I dragged a hand through my hair, exhaling hard. No turning back now.

"During that storm, when we got stuck..." I hesitated, then forced myself to say it. "Sophie and I... kissed."

Nate didn't react at first. Just stared at me, expression unreadable.

The usual clink of glasses and low hum of conversation from the bar faded into the background.

Nate's expression darkened as he processed my words.

"You kissed my sister."

Nate's voice was calm. Too calm. That dangerous kind of quiet before a storm.

I didn't flinch. Didn't look away. "I did."

No point in lying.

But I wasn't about to tell him everything, either.

Because this wasn't just about a kiss.

If Nate knew precisely how far things had gone— what Sophie had done, how she touched me, how she looked at me when she did it —he wouldn't just be looking at me like I'd betrayed him.

He'd be throwing punches.

"And I know I should've talked to you first," I admitted, keeping my voice steady. "But it just... happened."

Nate's jaw clenched the muscle ticking. "Just happened?" His eyes burned into mine. "She's my sister, Lucas. My little sister. And you're supposed to be my best friend. What the hell were you thinking?"

I leaned in, palms flat on the table. "Look, I never meant for this," I said. "But come on, Nate. Sophie's not some kid anymore. She's brilliant and fierce and completely her own person. And what I feel for her? I can't pretend it's nothing."

Nate's expression darkened as he exhaled sharply. "Real? You've known her for what—a couple days? And suddenly you have 'real feelings'?"

His laugh was short, bitter.

"This is Sophie we're talking about. My baby sister. The girl I've spent my whole life protecting."

I knew that.

I'd seen firsthand how much Nate cared about his family, how fiercely he looked out for Sophie—even from a distance.

And now, I was the one he'd never imagined needing to protect her from.

"Look, Nate, I get it. This whole thing blindsided you." I raised my hands, trying to keep my voice steady. "But Sophie isn't a little girl. She's a doctor, for Christ's sake. She deals with life and death every single day. Trust me, she knows her own mind and what she wants."

"And what, you think you're what's best for her?" Nate let out a harsh laugh, shaking his head. "Come on, Lucas. We both know your track record with relationships. How many times have I watched you lose interest and walk away when things got too serious?"

The hit landed hard, sharp, and direct, right where he knew it would hurt.

I clenched my jaw. "Nate, listen—"

"No."

The word cracked between us like a gunshot.

"You don't get to justify this," he said, his voice lower now, colder. "Sophie's off-limits, Lucas. End of story."

I opened my mouth, ready to fight for this, for her—but the words never came.

Because Nate was already standing, his chair scraping harshly against the floor.

The fury in his eyes wasn't just about me. It was about betrayal. About trust. About a line I'd crossed that he never thought I would.

"We're done here."

His voice was quiet, but the finality in it was deafening.

"Stay away from my sister, Lucas. I mean it."

Then he turned. Walked away like we were nothing more than strangers.

"Nate, wait!" I shot to my feet, knocking over my untouched beer.

He hesitated—just for a second.

His fingers wrapped around the brass door handle, and his body tensed like stone. I waited for a heartbeat, hoping he'd turn around and give me another chance to explain.

Instead, his shoulders squared.

Then he was gone.

The door clicked shut, leaving me stranded in the bar's dim light, chest tight, heart racing.

Deep down, I worried I'd just watched my best friend walk away for good.

I sank into my chair, dragging a shaky hand through my hair. I'd known this would go badly—but not like this.

Not like Nate looking at me like I'd put a knife in his back.

Not like watching the anger flicker into something colder, something that shut me out completely.

That part? That hit differently.

I exhaled hard and pulled out my phone. My thumb hovered over Sophie's name.

She deserved to know what had happened, but what the hell was I supposed to say?

Hey, your brother hates me now and forbade me from seeing you.

Yeah. That'd go over well.

I stared at the screen until it dimmed, then shoved the phone back into my pocket. Dragging Sophie into this mess right now wouldn't help anything. It would only make my headache worse.

I needed time. Needed to figure out my next move.

The bar suddenly felt too damn loud, too hot, too crowded. The walls closed in, my lungs seizing as my thoughts scattered. I slapped some cash onto the table and pushed through the crowd, barely registering the music, the chatter, the clink of glasses.

The night air hit like a shock of cold water, salt, and sea rushing into my lungs.

I took a long breath, letting the familiar scents of home wrap around me—jasmine from Mrs. Barlow's garden, fried fish from the pier, the briny scent of the bay. Usually, it grounded me.

Tonight, it barely made a dent.

I started walking. Didn't know where I was going at first; just needed to move. My boots scuffed against the worn sidewalk, the streetlights stretching long shadows across the damp pavement.

Fog rolled in, thick and low, swallowing up the town in its quiet grip.

I shoved my hands into my pockets, curling inward against the chill. Today had been relentless—Sophie, the crash site, Nate.

Too much.

Each step felt heavier, fatigue pressing on me like a physical weight.

I'd deal with everything in the morning.

Right now, I just needed sleep.

Chapter Six

♥

SOPHIE

The next morning, I stepped up to the nurses' station, flipping through a patient chart, but my mind was only half on the words in front of me. Sleep had been in short supply, and my coffee had barely made a dent in my exhaustion.

And then, I felt it.

That unmistakable presence.

Before I even looked up, I knew he was there.

Lucas.

I glanced up, my pulse hitching, when I saw him standing just a few feet away. He looked like hell—messy hair, dark circles under his eyes, tension etched into his jaw.

"Jesus, Lucas," I muttered, setting my chart down. "You look like you went ten rounds with insomnia and lost. Bad night?"

His gaze flickered, and for a moment, something unreadable passed over his face.

"You have no idea.," he admitted, rubbing the back of his neck. "Listen, can we talk somewhere private?"

The weight in his voice pulled me upright. My exhaustion faded, replaced by something sharper. Concern. Dread. A growing sense that whatever he was about to say, I wouldn't like it.

"Sure," I said, scanning the ER. "The on-call room should be empty."

I led the way, the familiar hum of the hospital fading as we stepped into the small, dimly lit space. The door clicked shut, and suddenly, the air felt different.

He was tense. More than tense.

I crossed my arms, watching him closely. "What's going on?"

Lucas dragged a hand through his already messy hair. "I talked to Nate last night." His voice was quiet. "About us."

A sharp inhale left my lips. "Oh."

I wasn't even sure what to say.

But Lucas's expression told me everything I needed to know.

"How did it go?" I asked, though I already knew the answer.

He winced. "Not well." A humorless chuckle left his throat. "Nate was... angry. Furious, actually. He told me to stay away from you."

Silence. A beat of disbelief. Then—pure, unfiltered anger.

"He what?" I snapped, stepping closer. "Who does he think he is, telling me who I can and can't see?"

"Sophie, he's just trying to protect you," Lucas said, but even he didn't sound convinced by the words.

I scoffed. "Protect me? Lucas, I'm not some delicate little thing that needs protection. I'm a grown woman. I make my own choices."

I took another step forward, anger simmering just beneath the surface—but as my eyes locked onto his, some of that fire melted into something else.

Something deeper.

Lucas exhaled sharply, shaking his head. "I know that. Believe me, I told him the same thing. But Nate... he'll never see you as anything but his little sister. You and me together? That wasn't in his big brother's playbook."

His voice was low and rough, and I could feel the weight of his words between us.

But there was something he wasn't saying.

I moved even closer, tilting my chin to look up at him. "What about you?" I asked, my voice quieter now.

Lucas's breath hitched, his gaze dropping to my lips briefly before snapping back up.

And just like that, the air changed.

The room shrank.

The space between us was practically nonexistent now, the unspoken tension pressing in on all sides.

Lucas didn't move away.

Neither did I.

"Sophie."

Lucas' voice was low, rough—like he was barely holding something back.

"What I feel for you... it's not hard to accept at all. That's what scares me."

His fingers caught a wayward curl, tucking it behind my ear before trailing down my cheek. His touch was gentle, almost worshipful like he was trying to commit every detail to memory.

"You're incredible," he murmured. "Brilliant. Fierce. Beautiful. I've never known anything like this."

A shiver ran through me at his words—not from the sentiment alone, but because I heard the raw honesty in his voice.

I pressed into his palm, my eyes closing briefly, surrendering to the moment.

When I looked at him again, there was no hesitation. No fear. Just fire.

"Then why are we letting Nate dictate what happens between us?" My voice was steady, but my heart pounded. "This is our decision, Lucas."

His jaw tightened, but his hand stayed on me, his thumb grazing my cheek.

"Sophie," he said, his breath unsteady, "you have to know how much I want this. Want you. But Nate's my best friend. I can't just ignore his feelings."

A frustrated breath left my lips. "So what, you're just going to let Nate decide for you?" I stepped closer. Close enough that the air between us crackled, thick with heat and tension.

"Tell me you don't feel this," I murmured, daring him to say it. "Tell me I'm imagining it."

Lucas swallowed hard, his restraint written in every tense line of his body. "I can't," he admitted, voice gruff. "But Nate is like a brother to me. The thought of losing his friendship..."

I softened. Just a little.

I understood that.

But that didn't mean I was letting him off the hook.

I reached up, fingers skimming his jaw, feeling the warmth of his skin beneath my touch. "Lucas, I get it—Nate means the world to you. Hell, he's my brother, and I love him too. But he doesn't own us. He doesn't get to decide who I choose."

I hesitated, my heart slamming against my ribs. The words teetered on the edge of my lips before I let them fall.

"I kept thinking about you last night."

Lucas' breath hitched, his fingers twitching at his sides.

I shouldn't have felt so bold, but how he looked at me made me braver.

"I tried to sleep, but every time I closed my eyes, I saw you." My voice dipped lower, not a whisper, but close. "I could feel your hands on me. Your lips..." I bit my bottom lip, watching his eyes darken and his breath shallow.

"It was driving me crazy."

Lucas' fists clenched, tension coiling through his muscles like he was one breath away from giving in.

I hesitated, my teeth sinking into my lower lip as I gathered the nerve to say it out loud. Then, finally, I let the truth spill between us, low and breathless.

"I couldn't stop thinking about you," I whispered, heat curling around every word. "I... I touched myself, imagining it was your hands on me instead."

Lucas inhaled sharply, his body tensing at my words. I could tell the image of me lying in bed, touching myself while thinking of him, sent a jolt of desire straight through him.

He groaned softly, his resolve crumbling. "God," he murmured, his voice rough with desire. "You can't say things like that and expect me to resist you."

"Then don't resist." My whisper barely filled the space between us, my breath warm against his lips. "I want you, Lucas. I've never wanted anyone the way I want you."

That was all it took.

A sharp inhale. A flicker of hesitation. And then—his control snapped.

With a low, guttural sound, Lucas' hands framed my face, his lips crashing against mine in a searing, desperate kiss.

"Christ, Sophie," he rasped between kisses, his voice thick with hunger. "I want you so much I can barely think straight."

Neither could I.

My hands fumbled with the door handle, finally locking it closed behind me, silencing the chaotic hum of the hospital beyond.

And then I turned—right into the intensity of Lucas' stare.

It hit me like a punch to the chest. The sheer weight of it, the way his dark eyes burned into mine, heavy with everything we'd been holding back.

I didn't hesitate.

In two steps, I reached him, my fingers twisting into his collar as I dragged him down into another fierce, breath-stealing kiss.

Lucas met me with equal force, hands diving into my curls, gripping, tilting my head just right as he deepened the kiss, devouring me like he'd been starving for this.

Because he had.

We both had.

Every sharp breath, every frantic movement was pure, unfiltered need. I felt his fingers slide down my back, dragging over my waist, gripping me like he needed something to anchor him.

My hands weren't any better—yanking at his belt, tugging it free with a clumsy desperation. Lucas' breath hitched, but he didn't stop me, his fingers diving beneath the hem of my scrubs, finding the drawstring, tugging.

We broke apart only long enough to shove away the last remaining barriers.

And then there was nothing between us.

Nothing but heat, tension, and the raw, reckless need building between us for far too long.

Lucas spun me around, bending me over the small table in the corner of the room. I braced myself against the cool surface, a soft gasp escaping me as Lucas ran his hands reverently down my sides.

Lucas groaned as I reached behind me to wrap my hand around his hard, hot length, stroking him with firm, purposeful motions.

"Lucas, please," I breathed. "I want you so much."

Lucas released a shaky breath as he reached for his wallet. He fumbled for a moment before extracting a small foil packet, the crinkle of the wrapper seeming impossibly loud in the quiet on-call room.

Lucas rolled the latex down his length with practiced ease, taking a moment to steady himself. I looked at him over my shoulder, and his eyes met mine. They were dark with desire, and his pupils were blown wide. A shiver ran through me at the intensity of his gaze.

"Lucas," I wasn't above begging at this point; I needed him inside me that badly. "Please!"

That single word broke the last of Lucas's restraint. He positioned himself at my entrance, gripping my hips as he rammed inside me. We both gasped at the exquisite sensation as he filled me completely and then some. Lucas paused for a moment, savoring the tight heat enveloping him.

"God, Sophie," he groaned, his voice rough with desire. "You feel incredible."

I pushed back against him, urging him deeper. "Move," I pleaded breathlessly. "Please, Lucas."

Lucas began to thrust, setting a steady rhythm that had me gripping the edge of the table. The small room filled with the sounds of our passion—skin against skin, breathy moans, and whispered words of encouragement.

I grabbed the table harder as Lucas hit a particularly sensitive spot. "Right there," I gasped. "Don't stop."

Lucas increased his pace, angling his hips to hit that spot again. I bit my lip to stifle my moans, acutely aware of the busy hospital beyond the thin walls.

Lucas leaned forward, his chest pressing against my back as he nuzzled my neck. His hot breath tickled my ear as he whispered, "Touch yourself for me, Sophie. I want to feel you come undone."

A shiver ran through me at his words. I slid one hand from the table, trailing it down my stomach until I reached the sensitive bundle of nerves between my legs. As I began to circle my clit with nimble fingers, Lucas groaned in approval.

"That's it," he murmured, his voice husky with arousal. "Show me how good it feels."

I gasped as the dual sensations overwhelmed me—Lucas's thick length stretching me deliciously while my own fingers sent sparks of pleasure radiating through my core. I could feel the tension building, coiling tighter with each stroke of Lucas's cock and each pass of my fingers. My breath came in short pants as I chased my release. Lucas's grip on my hips tightened, pulling me back to meet each thrust.

The coil of pleasure wound tighter and tighter, threatening to snap at any moment. Lucas's thrusts became more erratic, his breathing ragged against my neck. I could tell he was close, too.

"Sophie," he groaned, "I'm not gonna last much longer. Come for me, baby."

His words pushed me over the edge. Wave after wave of ecstasy crashed over me as my orgasm hit. My inner walls clenched around Lucas, pulling him deeper. I bit down on my lip to stifle my cries of pleasure, my body trembling with the intensity of my release.

Lucas followed moments later, burying himself to the hilt as he came with a muffled groan. His body shuddered against mine, his arms wrapping around my waist to hold me close as we rode out the aftershocks together.

For several long moments, we remained still, our bodies intertwined as we caught our breath. Lucas's forehead rested against my shoulder, his lips brushing my skin with each exhale. I could feel his heart pounding against my back, mirroring my own rapid pulse.

Slowly, reluctantly, Lucas eased out of me, eliciting a soft gasp from us both at the loss of connection. Lucas quickly disposed of the condom and helped me turn around, his hands gentle as he steadied me. My legs felt weak, trembling slightly in the aftermath.

Lucas cupped my face in his hands, his thumbs caressing my flushed cheeks as he gazed into my eyes. His gentle gaze made my pulse flutter. His kiss left me lightheaded, deep, and slow, stealing my breath and thoughts.

"You're gorgeous," he murmured, gentle fingers brushing back my hair. The tenderness in his touch was jarring after our frantic moments before.

My fingers traced lazy shapes on Lucas' chest, feeling the warmth beneath my touch. "Lucas, we need to talk to Nate together."

His muscles tensed beneath my touch, and a crease formed between his brows. "Sophie, I don't think that's wise. Nate made it pretty clear—"

"I know," I cut in softly. "But this stopped being just about you and Nate the moment *this* happened." I gestured between the two of us.

I stepped backward, pulling up my panties and scrub pants and attempting to tame my wild curls. "This isn't just some fling Nate can wish away." My eyes locked with Lucas'. "What we have matters. And I'm not giving up on it."

Lucas let out a heavy breath, pulling up his boxers and pants. The doubt was evident on his face. "Look, Sophie, I get it. But Nate's stubborn as hell - you know that. He still sees you as his little sister—someone he needs to protect."

I lifted my chin. "Then we'll make him see me as the woman I am." My voice was steady, unwavering. "I'm not a child, Lucas. I'm a doctor. I make my own decisions—about my life, about my relationships. Nate doesn't get to decide this."

Lucas' expression flickered with something unreadable before he let out a heavy sigh, raking a hand through his already messy hair.

"You're right," he said, his voice rough with resignation. "All this sneaking around... Nate should hear it from us. Both of us."

A slow, relieved smile tugged at my lips. "Thank you." I reached up, brushing my fingers against his cheek, savoring the warmth of his skin. "We'll face this together, okay?"

Lucas leaned into my touch like he needed it. "Together," he murmured.

We finished straightened our clothes, erasing the physical evidence of what happened. But nothing could erase the heat still simmering between us.

As I reached for the door handle, Lucas caught my wrist gently.

"Wait."

I turned back, brow lifting in question. He grabbed me before I could speak, pulling me into a kiss that was soft and deliberate, saying everything we couldn't put into words.

My breath caught when he finally drew back.

"For luck," he whispered.

I smiled and pulled the door open. "With our track record? We'll need all we can get."

Chapter Seven

♥

Lucas

The porch creaked under my boots as Sophie and I stood side by side, staring at the door in front of us. Nate's door.

I hated that it felt like walking into a fight.

The salty breeze from the bay stirred Sophie's copper curls, and before I could think better of it, I reached for her hand, giving it a quick squeeze.

She squeezed back.

Then the door swung open.

Nate's expression darkened the second he saw us. His gaze flicked between Sophie and me, sharp and unreadable.

"What are you doing here?" His voice was cold. Guarded.

I braced myself.

"We need to talk," Sophie said, her voice steady as she squared her shoulders. "All of us. Together."

For a second, I thought he might slam the door in our faces. Hell, part of me was surprised he hadn't already.

Instead, his jaw flexed, his nostrils flaring slightly before he exhaled. Then, with a sharp, reluctant jerk of his head, he stepped back.

Wordlessly, he let us in.

The tension in the living room was suffocating.

Nate stood firm, arms crossed, his stance radiating disapproval.

Sophie and I sat on the worn leather couch, but I might as well have been sitting on a live wire. My whole body was coiled, waiting for Nate to explode.

"Alright," he said gruffly, his glare fixed on me. "You wanted to talk. So talk."

Sophie inhaled deeply, her fingers fidgeting in her lap. I knew she was nervous, but her voice? Steady. Sure.

"Nate, I know you're upset about Lucas and me. But you have to understand—this isn't some fling or passing attraction. What we have is real."

Nate's jaw clenched. "Real? You've known each other for what, a week? How the hell can you possibly know it's real?"

I exhaled slowly, forcing myself to stay calm.

"Because I've never felt this way about anyone before," Sophie said, her voice quieter now. "Lucas understands me in a way no one else ever has. He challenges me. He makes me laugh. And we care about each other. Deeply."

Her hand found mine, fingers threading through mine like it was the easiest thing in the world.

I squeezed back, my thumb grazing over her knuckles.

"When I'm with him, I can be completely myself," Sophie continued, turning to look at me. "He sees me for who I am."

I swallowed hard, meeting her gaze, her words hitting deeper than I was ready for.

Then I turned back to Nate.

"I get why you're pissed," I said, my voice rough. "I know this isn't what you wanted. But what I feel for Sophie? It's real. She challenges me, inspires me—makes me want to step up and deserve her."

Nate's eyes flicked to our joined hands. His expression hardened.

"Right," he muttered, voice dripping with skepticism. "Until you get bored and move on to the next conquest. This isn't some game, Lucas. She's my sister."

There it was.

The part I'd been waiting for.

The part that cut the deepest.

The hit landed, but I didn't back down.

"You think I don't know that?" My voice was rough, steady. "This isn't like those other times."

I squeezed Sophie's hand again, her warmth steadying me.

"Yeah, I've messed up before—no point denying that. But with Sophie..." My chest grew tight as I struggled for words. "It's different. I can't imagine going back to how things were."

The thought alone made me ache.

Sophie met her brother's stare head-on. "I know what you're doing, Nate. Playing the protective big brother. But I don't need you fighting my battles anymore—I can handle my own life." Her voice softened, but her conviction never wavered. "And I want Lucas in it. He makes me happy. Simple as that."

Nate exhaled sharply, dragging a hand through his hair, frustration etched into every line of his body.

Silence stretched between us.

And then, Nate looked at us and, for the first time, really saw us.

Saw the way I held Sophie's hand like I'd never let go. Saw the way she leaned into me without hesitation.

His jaw tightened. Then, finally, he let out a long, grudging sigh.

"I still don't like this," he muttered, arms crossing over his chest. "But... I can see how much you care about each other."

Then his gaze snapped to me, hard and unyielding.

"If you hurt her, best friend or not, I'll break every bone in your body. Understood?"

I met his stare, unwavering. "I'd expect nothing less."

Sophie rolled her eyes, groaning. "I can take care of myself, you know."

Nate exhaled sharply, his expression softening for the first time. "I know." His voice was quieter now. "But you'll always be my little sister."

A pause. A flicker of hesitation.

Then, reluctantly, he nodded.

"If this is really what you both want... I won't stand in your way."

And just like that, everything changed.

Sophie's face lit up with pure joy as she launched herself at Nate, arms wrapping around him in a tight, fierce hug.

"Thank you," she murmured against his chest. "I love you, big brother."

Nate hesitated for half a second before his arms came up to return the embrace. His tough-guy act was slipping, but only a little.

Over Sophie's head, his eyes locked onto mine—sharp, serious. A warning.

"I mean it, man," he said gruffly. "You hurt her, and they'll never find your body."

I nodded, my expression just as serious. "I understand. And Nate... thank you. Your friendship means the world to me. I promise I'll do right by Sophie."

His scowl didn't disappear entirely, but something in his stance shifted. A little less tension, a little more reluctant acceptance.

"You better," he muttered, warmth creeping into his voice despite his best efforts.

Sophie pulled back, her eyes shimmering with unshed tears, but her smile was impossible to miss.

I watched them, feeling the weight of the past few days finally ease from my shoulders. It wasn't perfect—Nate's acceptance came with plenty of conditions—but it was something. And after everything, that was more than I could've asked for.

Sophie stepped back, dabbing at her eyes, and I moved beside her, pulling her in close like I'd been wanting to do all night. My arm settled naturally around her waist like it belonged there.

Her tear-filled eyes met mine, relief written across every inch of her face.

Some things didn't need words.

I leaned down, pressing a soft kiss to her forehead, letting it linger just a little too long.

Nate cleared his throat—loud enough to wake the dead.

"Right," he said, arms crossing as he leveled us with an unimpressed look. "I'm feeling generous today—mostly because no one ended up murdered—but I really don't need a front-row seat to..." He gestured vaguely between us. "...whatever this is."

He rolled his eyes for good measure.

Sophie laughed softly, her cheeks flushing as she stepped back just enough to appease him.

"Sorry, Nate," she said, though there was zero actual remorse in her tone.

Nate dragged a hand through his hair with an exaggerated sigh, shaking his head.

"I'm already regretting this."

But that half-smile tugging at his mouth?

That said otherwise.

***

Stepping out of Nate's house, I instinctively reached for Sophie's hand, lacing my fingers through hers. Holding her like this—out in the open, without secrecy or hesitation—felt damn good.

The setting sun washed the neighborhood in deep orange and soft pink hues, the breeze rolling in from the ocean sending loose strands of Sophie's red curls dancing around her face. I watched her tuck them behind her ear, and for a second, I forgot everything except how much I wanted to pull her in and kiss her again.

"That went better than I expected," Sophie said, squeezing my hand. "I thought Nate might actually take a swing at you for a minute there."

I chuckled, pulling her closer against my side as we walked toward my truck. "Honestly? I wouldn't have blamed him if he did. But I'm glad he's willing to give us a chance."

We stopped beside my old blue pickup, and I turned to face her.

"So," I said, shifting slightly, unable to keep the grin off my face. "Where do we go from here?"

Sophie studied me for a long moment, her fingers brushing lightly along my jaw, a quiet kind of certainty in her touch.

"Wherever we want," she murmured, her voice soft but sure. "Together."

A slow warmth spread through my chest. I reached up, lacing my fingers through hers, holding her hand against my cheek like I could make the moment last forever. The scent of jasmine mixed with salt on the breeze, and the last streaks of sunlight set her copper hair ablaze.

I let out a breath, my voice low. "Together sounds perfect."

And with Sophie standing there, looking at me like that, I knew—for the first time in a long time—I was exactly where I was meant to be.

Epilogue

♥

SOPHIE

The Rusty Anchor hummed with its usual evening crowd—glasses clinking, warm laughter floating through the air, and the steady, familiar rhythm of conversation blending into the background. The scent of salt and old timber wrapped around me, grounding me in the place that had become so much more than just another bar.

I curled my fingers around my ginger ale, letting the fizzy warmth settle as I leaned into Lucas. His arm rested lazily over my shoulder, his fingertips grazing the loose braid draped over my shoulder like he couldn't resist the touch.

"You've got that look again," I teased, tilting my head just enough to meet his gaze.

"What look?" His grin was slow, easy—completely Lucas.

"The one that says you're about to say something cheesy."

Lucas chuckled, shifting closer. "I was just going to say... this moment right here? My favorite place to be."

A laugh bubbled from my chest as I let my head fall against his shoulder. Cheesy. Absolutely. But I couldn't deny that it settled something deep inside me.

Across the table, Nate swirled the whiskey in his glass, his gaze flicking toward the door every few minutes. His usual gruff exterior was firmly in place, but something about the way his shoulders tensed made me narrow my eyes.

"You waiting for someone?" I asked, taking a slow sip of my drink.

Nate scoffed. "I don't wait for anyone."

Lucas and I exchanged a glance—oh, this was going to be good.

Before I could press further, the door swung open, and a gust of cool night air swept inside. A tall woman strode in, unwinding a scarf from her neck, her sharp silver-blue eyes scanning the room with keen precision.

I didn't recognize her, but judging by the way Nate instantly went stiff as a board, he did.

"Tessa," he muttered, barely loud enough to hear.

Lucas leaned forward, clearly entertained. "Friend of yours?"

"Not exactly," Nate said, though his tone was anything but indifferent.

Tessa's gaze landed on him, cool and assessing, and in that instant, it was apparent—she knew exactly what kind of effect she had on him.

She strode over, confidence in every measured step, her dark hair spilling down her back in a sleek sheet. "Detective Whitaker," she greeted smoothly, setting her leather satchel on our table. "You've been avoiding me. I'm here to talk about the burglaries."

Nate's jaw tightened. "It's still an active investigation."

Tessa's lips curved like she was used to people being difficult—but rarely letting it stop her. "Well then, looks like I'll need to stick around and do some investigating."

I bit back a grin as Lucas draped an arm over my chair, leaning in conspiratorially. "They won't last a week before the sparks fly."

I tilted my head, pretending to consider it. "Maybe less."

As Tessa ordered a drink and Nate tried (and failed) to ignore her, Lucas kissed my temple.

"Think they'll figure it out as fast as we did?" he murmured.

"Not a chance," I said, laughing softly as I curled into him.

The Rusty Anchor hummed around us, a steady heartbeat of warmth and familiarity. And as the night stretched on, I knew one thing for sure.

I'd finally found my anchor.

***

Dear Reader,

Thank you so much for reading *On Call for You*! I hope you loved Lucas and Sophie's story as much as I loved writing it. Their journey—from forbidden attraction to undeniable love—was filled with tension, heart, and plenty of heat, and I'm so grateful you came along for the ride.

If you enjoyed the book, I'd truly appreciate it if you took a moment to leave a review. Reviews help authors like me reach more readers, and they mean the world when it comes to sharing these stories. Even a few words can make a huge difference!

Thank you for your support, and I can't wait to share more love stories with you!

With gratitude, Hana York

***

Ready for more?

If you loved *On Call for You*, you won't want to miss what's coming next! *Investigating Desire* is a sizzling, small-town, grumpy/sunshine romance featuring Nate Whitaker—a brooding detective who's sworn off love after a brutal divorce—and Tessa Donovan, a sharp, relentless investigator who refuses to back down, especially when it comes to Nate.

When a high-stakes case forces them to work together, their clashing personalities ignite more than just frustration. Tessa is all fire and determination, while Nate is convinced he's done with love for good. But the more they push each other away, the harder it becomes to deny the heat between them.

Will Nate risk his guarded heart for the one woman who refuses to give up on him? Or will his past keep him from the future he never saw coming?

Keep reading for a sneak peek at Chapter One of *Investigating Desire*, available March 11, 2025 on Amazon!!

Sneak Peak
of Investigating
Desire

♥

Nate

Dawn broke over the crime scene, the early light catching the jagged edges of broken glass scattered across the sidewalk. I stood still, letting the weight of another robbery press against the already tense muscles in my shoulders. Through the smashed storefront window, I spotted an overturned cash register, receipts, and loose bills littering the floor like discarded confetti. A mess. Like every other damn break-in this month.

I yanked out my notepad, scribbling the exact details I'd written five times before. New location, identical story: no sign of forced entry, zero leads worth following. Another case destined for the unsolved pile.

"Detective Whitaker?"

The sharp, self-assured voice sliced through the background noise of radio static and cop chatter. I exhaled slowly, bracing myself for yet another store owner demanding answers I didn't have. But when I turned, I was met with something else entirely.

She stood just beyond the yellow tape, all poise and sharp angles—long black hair falling well past her shoulders, piercing silver-blue eyes locking onto mine with a mix of determination and something that looked suspiciously like amusement. In her hand, a notepad and pen, held like a weapon.

"Tessa Donovan," she said, stepping forward like she belonged here. "I'm the journalist assigned to shadow you for the piece on law enforcement and the recent robberies."

Shadow me? My grip on the notepad tightened as I let my gaze flick from her face to the press badge clipped to her coat.

I didn't take the hand she extended. "Shadow me?" I said flatly, making no effort to hide my irritation.

"That's right." Her voice was smooth, unbothered by my less-than-welcoming tone. "I'm here to capture the human side of the investigation. The public loves to see the story behind the badge."

I snorted, shaking my head as I went back to my notes. "Great. That's exactly what we need—more people in the middle of a crime scene."

"I don't need your permission to do my job," she shot back, unfazed. "Just access. Which, by the way, your captain already approved."

I stopped writing mid-sentence, my jaw ticking. "Of course he did," I muttered under my breath.

I glanced back at her. She watched me closely, the corners of her lips tilted slightly like she knew I was two seconds from telling her to take her notepad and shove it.

"Look, Ms. Donovan, this isn't a PR stunt," I said, keeping my voice even. "It's a crime scene."

"And I'm not looking for PR," she countered, stepping closer, her boots crunching over the glass. "I'm here for authenticity. That means being where the action is and watching the people who do the real work. That's you, in case I wasn't clear."

A flicker of something twisted in my chest—annoyance, mostly. But also something grudgingly close to respect. She didn't scare easily; I'd give her that.

I met her gaze, letting the silence stretch between us. "Fine," I said finally. "Observe all you want. But don't get in my way, and don't expect me to slow down to explain things."

She smiled, flipping open her notepad like she'd already won. "Wouldn't dream of it," she murmured, pen moving fast across the page.

I sighed, already regretting every single life choice that led to this moment.

This was going to be a long damn assignment.

Tessa dusted a few flecks of dust from her jeans, utterly unfazed by the chaos around her. "So, Detective," she said, her voice smooth, confident. "What's your read on this scene?"

I hesitated, watching her. Most reporters would have come in with their own half-baked theories, fishing for a quote to spin whatever angle they wanted. But her eyes held something different—genuine curiosity. Against my better judgment, I answered.

"Smash and grab," I muttered, waving a hand at the mess. "Amateur hour. They left evidence all over the place."

She jotted something down, nodding. "Connected to the other break-ins?"

"Can't say yet," I said, stepping toward the register.

As I moved, I caught the faintest trace of her perfume—something savory. I ignored how it tugged at the edges of my awareness, forcing my focus back on the scene.

"What's your take?" The words left my mouth before I could stop them.

Tessa blinked, clearly surprised. "You're actually asking me?"

I shrugged. "You're here. Might as well see if you've got anything useful to add."

Her pen drummed against the notepad as she sized me up, considering the invitation. After a moment's deliberation, she moved beside me with that same confident precision, taking care not to disturb anything at the scene.

"Well, since you're curious..." She crouched slightly, tracing the air above the debris. "See how the glass sprayed outward? That means they broke it from the inside."

My eyebrows lifted slightly. "Pretty sharp for a reporter."

Tessa shot me a half smile that said she knew exactly how good she was at her job. "Been around enough crime scenes," she said lightly, but I didn't miss the note of satisfaction in her voice.

Our eyes met, and the space between us shifted.

I knew that feeling. That unwanted pull, the one that crept up when you least expected it, the one I'd buried under long work hours and a firm no-relationships policy.

I cleared my throat and looked away first, dragging my attention back to the register.

This was a distraction I didn't need. A distraction with sharp blue eyes and a habit of pushing her way into things. I had a caseload stacked a mile high, a city full of criminals who didn't seem to take a damn night off, and a personal life I'd long since given up trying to fix.

The last thing I needed was some smart-mouthed journalist getting under my skin.

And yet, as I scanned the ransacked shop, my gaze kept finding her. The way she bit her lower lip in concentration while scribbling notes. How the early morning light caught subtle hints of silver in her dark hair. The way she tilted her head, completely focused, like she was trying to see past the obvious.

I exhaled sharply, forcing myself to look anywhere else.

Nope. Not happening.

I'd sworn off love for a reason. And no amount of sharp wit and striking blue eyes would make me forget that.

I exhaled sharply, shaking my head. Get it together, Whitaker.

I crouched near the register, studying a deep scuff mark on the floor. "Something heavy hit here," I muttered, more to myself than anyone else.

Before I could process it, she was right there, dropping to a knee beside me. Close. Too close.

Her shoulder brushed mine, and my breath caught. Her scent—subtle but intoxicating—wrapped around me, warm and lingering.

"Could be from the register when they knocked it over," she murmured, voice low, close to my ear.

My jaw tightened. "Possibly." The word came out rougher than I intended.

I needed to move. To put space between us before I started wondering Tessa tasted like.

Clearing my throat, I straightened. "We'll need to dust for prints here," I said, gesturing to the scuff mark, forcing my focus back where it belonged.

She stood too, moving with an ease that only made it worse. She was still close, still watching me. Her body heat seeped through my shirt, and the air between us suddenly thick.

I met her eyes—striking, impossible to ignore. Something flickered there, something unreadable. My pulse kicked up.

Her lips parted like she was about to say something, but before she could, my radio crackled to life, shattering whatever the hell was happening between us.

I stepped back fast, like I'd been caught with my hand in the candy jar. "I should check in with forensics," I said gruffly, turning away.

She took her time following suit, and when I glanced back, there was something annoyingly smug in the curve of her mouth.

"You okay there, Detective?" she asked, voice laced with amusement. "You seem a bit... flustered."

I scowled. "I'm fine."

"Of course," she mused, tapping her pen against her notepad.

The warmth in my neck spread up to my ears. I gritted my teeth, attacking my notepad with my pen, pretending I hadn't just let myself get tangled up in something dangerous.

Because whatever that was between us?

It wasn't happening.

Fuck, I was in trouble.

Investigating Desire will be available March 11, 2025 on Amazon!!

Hana York Books

♥

Hearts on Duty Series

Sparks of Temptation

Love's Anchor

On Call for You

Investigating Desire

For a full list of titles, please visit Hana York's website

www.HanaYork.com

About the Author

♥

Hana York writes fast-paced, heart-pounding contemporary romance packed with irresistible heroes, strong heroines, laugh-out-loud banter, and just the right amount of spice to keep things sizzling. Her books are for readers who love grumpy men falling hard, fierce women who don't need saving, and the kind of chemistry that sparks off the page.

When she's not crafting stories full of love, tension, and toe-curling moments, you'll find her daydreaming about small-town charm, plotting ridiculous meet-cutes, and consuming an unhealthy amount of coffee. She believes in happily-ever-afters, overprotective heroes who don't stand a chance against their heroines, and that every great love story should come with a side of sass.

If you love forced proximity, off-limits attraction, sizzling tension, and romance that makes your heart race, welcome to the world of Hana York!

Follow Hana York for new releases, exclusive content, and behind-the-scenes fun! Visit www.HanaYork.com for more!